Author Dedication:

For Stuart and Cameron.
Many thanks for your love and
understanding during times the Navy
sent your own sailor dad to sea.
~ R.H.M.

~

Illustrator Dedication:

To my dad, Brown Jarboe,
a World War II veteran.
~ M.J.

My Sailor Dad

Written by

Ross H. Mackenzie

Illustrated by

Marvin Jarboe

PATRIOT KIDS®
Little Books. Big Ideas.

www.patriot-kids.com

My daddy's a sailor on big Navy ships! He travels the world when

...oes on his trips.

He's worked with all kinds of the ships that they sail – from huge ones [
Destroyers and frigates and submarines too; patrol boats, large amphib

nall ones the size of a whale.
1d cruisers fight true.

There even are special boats
Navy SEALs use
To fight their tough missions
without leaving clues.

He's swabbed dirty decks   and he's cleaned out big guns –

and some of those guns can weigh up to four tons!

He worked on a carrier not long ago –
and saw all the jets as they zoomed by so low!

Some friends on that ship work with choppers and planes,
and working on planes can be hard, he explains.

One day I went with him to his Navy base.
It really is quite a remarkable place!
The ships are all parked side-by-side
on the pier –
they have giant ropes that
are holding them near.
I stood there and looked up
at one of the boats
and couldn't believe that it actually floats!

I saw tons of things on the ship that were co
I saw shiny guns, plus the huge anchor chai

ome stuff that I never would see at my school!
range radars, long missiles – and even a crane.

I saw a big helo chained dow
That day was terrific I spent wi

the deck; I even said, "Hi!" to a maintenance tech!
y dad! We had a great time in the time that we had!

Sometimes in the Navy my dad goes to sea,
and I know he's sad when he has to leave me.

My mommy has told me sometimes throug
He goes overseas to make everythir

er tears that Daddy is working when he disappears.
ght; he really is kind of a modern-day knight!

He fights for our freedom, he fights for the poo
He fights to help people in countries out the

fights against people whose hearts are not pure.
and up for their rights so they don't live in fear.

So just 'cause he's not here to kiss me goodnigh

bes not mean that everything won't be all right.

I know that he's out there at sea working har
He loves me at home and he lov

rotecting us all while he's standing the guard.
e at sea – I'm glad he's a sailor . . .

Ross H. Mackenzie • Author

Ross H. Mackenzie graduated from the U.S. Naval Academy with a degree in English Literature. He also earned a Master's from St. John's College (Annapolis) and attended Harvard's Kennedy School of Government.

A former Navy pilot, Mr. Mackenzie deployed multiple times on eight different ships to many parts of the world during his 20-year military career. While in the Navy, Mr. Mackenzie taught English literature and writing at the U.S. Naval Academy for four years.

Mr. Mackenzie finds his passions in wide open spaces as an avid cyclist, hiker, and sportsman. He is a devoted father and husband and makes his home in Florida.

Mr. Mackenzie's other books include:
• *Brief Points: An Almanac for Parents and Friends of U.S. Naval Academy Midshipmen* (U. S. Naval Institute Press, 2004).
• *My Soldier Dad* (Patriot Kids, LLC, 2017)
• *Tying Up Water and Other Stories* (Amazon, 2012)
• *My Peaceful Dad* (Amazon, 2012)

Marvin Jarboe • Illustrator

A Kentucky native, Marvin Jarboe joined the Army in 1968 and served as an 81E20 Illustrator. He also earned a Bachelor of Fine Arts degree from Western Kentucky University.

Mr. Jarboe works in advertising, fine art, commercial screen printing, and stained glass.